WILLIAM SHAKESPEARE'S

The Tempest

Retold by Franzeska G. Ewart

Illustrated by David Wyatt

A & C Black • London

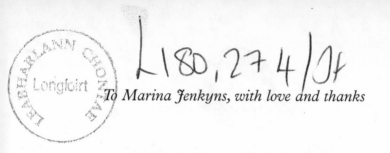

L180,274/04

To Marina Jenkyns, with love and thanks

White Wolves Series Consultant: Sue Ellis,
Centre for Literacy in Primary Education

This book can be used in the White Wolves Guided Reading
programme with experienced readers in Year 6

First published 2007 by
A & C Black Publishers Ltd
38 Soho Square, London, W1D 3HB

www.acblack.com

Text copyright © 2007 Franzeska G. Ewart
Illustrations copyright © 2007 David Wyatt

The rights of Franzeska G. Ewart and David Wyatt to be
identified as author and illustrator of this work respectively
have been asserted by them in accordance with the
Copyrights, Designs and Patents Act 1988.

ISBN 0-7136-8528-X
ISBN 978-0-7136-8528-2

A CIP catalogue for this book is available from the British Library.

Contents

List of characters

Alonso, *King of Naples*
Sebastian, *his brother*
Ferdinand, *Alonso's son*
Prospero, *a magician and rightful Duke of Milan*
Miranda, *his daughter*
Antonio, *Prospero's brother, the usurping Duke of Milan*
Ariel, *an airy spirit*
Caliban, *a savage and deformed slave*
Gonzalo, *an honest old councillor*
Adrian and Francisco, *lords*
Trinculo, *a jester*
Stephano, *a drunken butler*

Iris
Ceres   *represented by nymphs*
Juno

4

Act One

All hail, great master! Grave sir, hail! I come
To answer thy best pleasure; be't to fly,
To swim, to dive into the fire, to ride
On the curled clouds. To thy strong bidding
task
Ariel and all his quality.

Those were the first words I spoke to my master, Prospero, on that magical day – the day of the tempest. I'm sure you'll agree they were brave words indeed!

I knew, you see, that the day was going to be special. From the moment it dawned, the whole island seemed to hold its breath. The air hardly moved, and it felt as if every plant, every animal, and every spirit was waiting silently...

You've heard of 'the calm before the storm'. That's what it was like. We all knew that very soon Prospero would raise his mighty staff, and the sun would disappear. Then the wind would begin to howl, and the island would be filled with a magic more powerful than any it had ever seen before. So it was no wonder that I, Ariel, was willing to do anything, however dangerous, to make that happen.

My job, you see, was to carry out Prospero's spells and, believe me, I was *brilliant* at it! You'll soon see how brilliant, because I've come back to this beautiful island, where it all happened, to tell you. Listen well, for you're about to hear the story of *The Tempest* – a tale of love, and adventure, and murder plots, and *magic*.

Now, before you say you've heard a hundred magic stories, let me tell you that this magic was no ordinary sorcery. Oh no – it was in a class of its own! For the enchantments that took place on that day were so powerful that they changed everyone who fell under their spell. No one's life was ever the same again.

My life wasn't the same again, either, for in those few hours I gained something that's more important than life itself. After years and years of being a slave, I gained my freedom. Which is why, today, I could hop onto the back of a bat and fly here – back to this island paradise that for so long was my prison.

Did you see me swooping above, holding handfuls of black bat-hair in my fists and waving down at you? Did you hear me, singing at the top of my wild and wonderful voice?

No – I thought not! You didn't see or hear a thing, and how could you? To catch a glimpse of me, you have to have the eyes to see, and that means *magical* eyes. For I, Ariel, am an airy spirit, as my name tells you. And, since I'm sure you've never met anyone like me, let me try to explain.

Being an airy spirit means that my body is made of air, unlike yours, which is flesh and blood and bones. Where you walk on two legs, I fly, and dive, and hover, and soar. And where you are stuck, your whole life long, with one body, which hardly changes except to grow old and die, I live for ever; and I take as many different shapes as I like. I can be as huge as the greatest wave, or as tiny as the lowliest barnacle. I can have the most beautiful form imaginable, or the most hideous. I can also be invisible.

Come close and look at me now. I've made myself very tiny and curled up among the petals of a cowslip flower, so I'm powdered pollen yellow. My eyes are heavy with perfume and I'm holding them tight shut, for I'm listening to those words of mine again. They're echoing in my memory now, drowning out the pounding of the waves and the seabirds' cries, taking me – and you – back to that magical day: the day of the tempest.

At that time, my master Prospero was the ruler of the island, and the greatest magician who ever lived. But, powerful as Prospero's magic was, he still needed spirits to help him carry it out, and there was no spirit more able and willing than me.

Of course, I did have my 'gang' to help me. Prospero may have been my master, but I was in charge of a whole band of spirits who did as *I* commanded them! We carried out spectacular sorcery together, but the star of Prospero's magic shows was always *me*. And the show that began this story was the tempest, the sea-storm.

Prospero had been planning that storm ever since he and his daughter, Miranda, had arrived on the island. And when I tell you that Miranda was two when they were shipwrecked, and on that day she was a beautiful young woman of fourteen, you'll realise just how long that plan had taken.

Prospero and Miranda, you see, had not *chosen* to live their lives in a humble cave on an almost-deserted island with only sea-sounds to bring comfort to their ears. Would a duke, used to living in a palace in the fine city of Milan, with rich furniture and servants, *choose* to raise his little daughter far away from civilisation and the company of others?

For indeed, my master Prospero was a duke! In fact, he was Duke of Milan – the greatest state in Italy, which he had governed for many years. When I met him, though, his dukedom was just a memory; his royal gowns, his hat and his rapier were all stored away at the back of his cave. And instead of robes of office, he wore a magic cloak.

So of course this island life was not chosen. Prospero and Miranda's banishment from Milan was the result of a wicked plot, and when I tell you that this plot was hatched by none other than Prospero's own brother, you'll understand that we're dealing with real evil. And real evil, as anyone knows, can only be matched by real, powerful magic.

Antonio was the name of that wicked brother. Antonio, who'd looked on enviously as Prospero ruled Milan. Antonio, who'd helped his aging brother more and more with his government, and been trusted to do so. Antonio, who had eventually wanted to be Duke of Milan himself…

At last this ambition grew so strong that he drew up a treacherous plan. With the help of two other power-hungry villains – Alonso, the King of Naples, and Alonso's brother Sebastian – Antonio arranged for Prospero to be captured and bundled into a boat and pushed out to sea.

And, as if that wasn't cold-hearted enough, those wicked men sent his baby girl with him! Imagine it – until that day, Miranda had had everything a child could ask for, and a host of maidservants to look after her. Now, her bed was a wooden board with the sky for its canopy; and the sea sang her lullabies.

Perhaps you're wondering why Antonio didn't simply arrange to have his brother murdered? After all, he obviously cared less than nothing for him. Does that act of mercy reveal a tiny shell of goodness on the bare seabed that is Antonio's soul?

I'm sorry to say, it doesn't. The only reason Antonio spared his brother's life was that Prospero's subjects would have torn him limb from limb if they had suspected him of murdering their duke. For Prospero may not have been the best ruler Milan had ever had – it was rumoured that he spent rather more time in his library, poring over his books, than he did on affairs of state – but, all the same, he was dearly loved by his people. He told me so himself, and I always believed what my master said.

Now I'm not made of flesh and blood. I don't concern myself with all the stupidity that men call 'human life'. But, when I see how a brother can treat his own flesh and blood, I tell you – it makes me thankful I'm air-born!

Prospero and Miranda would have surely died on the open sea, had it not been for one man – a kind nobleman from Naples called

Gonzalo. Gonzalo risked his life to make sure Prospero had plenty of clothes, and food and drink, for himself and his child.

And Gonzalo wasn't only kind and noble. He was wise. He knew that food and drink weren't enough for Prospero's survival, and that without nourishment for his *soul* he would surely die. So Gonzalo filled that rotten carcass of a boat with books from his lord's library, and when at last Prospero and Miranda were washed up on the sands of this island, they had everything they needed in order to live. Not only that – with his magic books, and his magic staff, and his magic cloak, Prospero had everything he needed in order to take revenge on his unworthy brother.

And now, I hope, you can see how my story's beginning to take shape...

Prospero, you understand, was determined to get his dukedom back one day. But how on earth could he do that, living as he did on a deserted island? The only way was to use sorcery. And so for twelve years he studied his magic books, and he planned, and he waited, and when, one night, he read in the stars that all his enemies were due to sail past this island, he summoned me. He opened up the magic book and, as he showed me what I was to do, it was as if the very pages howled and roared and lashed their sea-fury at us!

For I was to whip up the calm, blue sea into the most violent storm ever seen. I, Ariel, was to become the tempest that would shipwreck the royal fleet with King Alonso, Antonio and Sebastian aboard. Their long and joyful voyage – for they had been to Tunisia to celebrate the marriage of King Alonso's daughter Claribel to an African king – was to come to a terrible end!

But I had to be careful. Even though my tempest was to be a storm to end all storms, the royal party was not to be drowned. That wasn't what my noble master wanted at all. Antonio, Alonso and Sebastian may have been willing to send Prospero and Miranda out on the open sea to almost certain death, but the revenge Prospero planned wasn't nearly so simple. And, as you listen to my story, you'll see how clever it was.

Oh, how the thought of that first spell thrilled me! I was on fire with enthusiasm as I flew off to carry it out. But, of course, although *I* was going to do all the roaring and foaming and thrashing and burning, it was Prospero who was actually in charge. It was *his* master plan, and it was perfect.

Now, as I told you, Prospero never intended to harm any of the people aboard the ships. For one thing, he had other ideas – death by drowning was far too good for his three enemies! But there was another reason why he'd given me strict instructions not to harm a single soul: not everyone aboard the royal ship was evil. There was Gonzalo, that wise, kind man whose actions had saved the lives of Prospero and Miranda; and there was Ferdinand, Alonso's fine young son, and heir to his throne.

So when I began to whip up the waves around the royal ship in preparation for the most terrifying storm those voyagers had ever seen, I knew I'd have to make sure that not one hair on their heads was harmed, and that not one single stain was left on their clothes. I told you it was a magical tempest, didn't I! Here's what I did:

I boarded the king's ship. Now on the beak,
Now in the waist, the deck, in every cabin,
I flamed amazement.

Yes indeed – I ripped through that ship like wildfire. From one end of the deck to the other I roared, splitting into a dozen pieces to engulf cabin after cabin with my fury.

Oh, I did enjoy that tempest. I was in my element! You should have heard those royal passengers, howling louder than the storm-winds themselves. For they thought their last hour had come – and what a nuisance they were to the sailors. In the end, the boatswain had to order them off the deck. Imagine – a common sailor giving orders to a king!

And it wasn't just the king and courtiers who were terrified of your Ariel. Even the sailors, who had spent all their lives at sea, were scared out of their wits. They didn't know where to look next, for no sooner had I struck the deck with my fire-fury than I was up above them on the mast, raining down thunderbolts on their helpless heads.

Who could blame them for taking a few nips of rum to calm their shattered nerves? I'll swear even Neptune, the king of the sea, was so terrified that his trident shook! But of course I never forgot what Prospero had instructed me, not for an instant. I knew I had to drive everyone except the sailors off the ship and make sure they landed safely in groups on the island, so that's what I did.

Not that it took much to persuade them to leave. The first man to leap into the wild sea was Ferdinand, and he was a sight to behold with his hair standing up on end like wet, shiny reeds.

Hell is empty, he yelled as he jumped, *and all the devils are here!*

And sure enough, it must have seemed like hell to everyone on board. A sea-storm is bad enough, but a sea-storm that soaks and burns at the same time is the stuff of nightmares. My spiriting was pure theatre – with Ariel as the leading light!

But all good things must come to an end. Eventually, I calmed myself and led everyone ashore, making sure that Ferdinand was in a special, sheltered place on his own. And if I could feel pity, I would have pitied that young man – for he thought he was the only survivor of the storm, and the poor thing was a sorry sight to see.

But magic-makers can't afford to waste time feeling sorry for their subjects. I went back to the ship, put the sailors to sleep (which wasn't difficult because they were exhausted), and sent the rest of the fleet on to Naples. I could imagine them arriving home, bursting to tell everyone about the terrible storm that had drowned their king, all his courtiers, and his handsome young son!

Then, at last, at two o'clock that afternoon, I *thought* I was finished. I was sure the tempest was to be my last spell for Prospero.

How wrong I was! I wasn't finished. Nothing like finished. And when Prospero told me that there was more to do, and the next four hours would be busier than ever, I'm afraid I thoroughly lost my temper. You should have heard the way I stood up to him. I was quite fearless in my fury.

I should have known better than to rage at Prospero though, for when I called him the 'greatest magician who ever lived', I didn't exaggerate. Prospero's magic was stronger than the magic of the most powerful gods, and no one knew that better than I did...

Act Two

When Prospero arrived on this island, I was not the airy spirit I am now. Oh dear me no – quite the reverse. I was trapped in the most hideous prison, and he was the only one with magic strong enough to rescue me. But no sooner had he given me my liberty than he made me his slave. He forced me to do his spriting, and I had no choice but to agree. For Prospero rescued me from a fate far, far worse than death.

He rescued me from Sycorax.

Oh, how that name fills me with horror, even now! Sycorax, you see, was a powerful, evil witch. She'd been banished to this island from Algeria, and they'd sent her away because of her unspeakably horrible spells. She was pregnant when she arrived (some say the father was the Devil!), and it was here that her son Caliban was born and still lives.

Now, at the time of Sycorax's banishment I was her slave. She had me in her power, and I won't tell you the things she wanted me to do, for they are far too vile to speak about. So vile, in fact, that one day I'd had enough – for I am a sensitive soul, despite my airiness. I couldn't do her mischief any longer, and I refused. I knew I would face a dreadful punishment, but nothing, I thought, could be more soul-destroying than making evil for that witch.

How wrong I was.

Can you imagine the worst punishment anyone could give an airy spirit? Sycorax gave it to me. Bristling with fury at my defiance, she opened up a pine tree and bundled me inside. Then she knotted me into that dark, dank trunk, forcing me to become as still and as hard as the wood itself. My lightness was all gone and in its place was sap-filled darkness.

That prison was worse than unbearable. And then, as if that wasn't bad enough, Sycorax died! That stone-hearted hag left me to eternal damnation.

Think of it. I, who love to hear the wind blow and the birds sing, locked in silence broken only by my own cries of despair. I, who live for the warmth of the sun and the light of the moon, locked in darkness blacker than the blackest night. And I, whose greatest joy is to glide and swoop, to dance in and out of the clouds, knotted into a wooden prison, unable to move.

For twelve long years I stayed there, thinking I would never get out. So, when Prospero arrived and heard my groans and used his magic to free me, is it any wonder I agreed to be his slave? And, although I never wanted to be under anyone's control again, my new life as Prospero's servant was far better than all those awful years with Sycorax. For every one of Prospero's spells was a work of art and, even if it didn't always seem to be, was cast for a good purpose. I may have moaned when I thought he worked me too hard, but carrying out his enchantments was always a pleasure.

Oh yes, I took great pride in my work, and – if an airy spirit can love – I loved my master. I respected him, too, for I knew that if I refused to do as he asked, I would be back inside another, bigger tree – with *no* hope of rescue! And so, after the tempest, when Prospero told me to prepare for the next spell, I calmed myself down and did as I was told.

This spell was to be a gentler affair; for it was a love-spell, and its young victim – King Alonso's son Ferdinand – was to be enchanted by the greatest gift I possess.

My *music*.

Here's the song I sang to Ferdinand, as he sat thinking sadly about his poor father. If he didn't quite believe Alonso was drowned, then this song made sure he did. And that, of course, was exactly what Prospero wanted.

Full fathom five thy father lies;
Of his bones are coral made;
Those are pearls that were his eyes;
Nothing of him that doth fade
But doth suffer a sea-change
Into something rich and strange.

It's good, isn't it? Do you hear how I made him think his father was not only dead, but turned into coral and pearl? Part of the ocean, just like me. I liked that, for it sweetened his sadness a little, and turned his thoughts to magic.

The spell worked, of course. That young man was spellbound by my music – for Ariel's music enchants everyone who has the ears to hear it. Oh yes, I tied him with that music as strongly as if its notes had been cords. I used no force against him, yet he was my willing prisoner.

And he couldn't even see me! Prospero had

ordered me to become invisible for this spell, to blend in with the sand and the sea, so that's exactly what I did. Using only my wonderful music, I led Ferdinand to Miranda, and then I made him fall in love with her, and she with him.

What a love-trap that was! Honey-sweet, and honey-smooth – but still as sticky a trap as ever was set. And all the while, I was as invisible as a sea-breeze.

Not that I really needed to be invisible. Ferdinand and Miranda wouldn't have seen me even if I had changed myself into a huge blue whale, for straightaway those young people only had eyes for each other. Here's what Miranda said about Ferdinand when she saw him:

I might call him
A thing divine; for nothing natural
I ever saw so noble.

I ask you! An ordinary-looking fellow, and she thought he looked like a god! What fools this 'love' makes of you humans. And Miranda wasn't the only one to see things through a haze of magic. Ferdinand was every bit as enchanted.

Most sure, the goddess
On whom these airs attend!

was what *he* said.

Ah, young love! Not that I pretend to understand it, for it's a human emotion that means nothing to me. Airy spirits aren't bound by such forces, for what's love but a prison?

Prospero, of course, was delighted to see his plan working perfectly. He wanted, more than anything, for his daughter to marry King Alonso's son. That way, one day she'd be Queen of Naples. There had always been a feud between Milan and Naples, you see, and that was the only sure way to end it. At last Milan and Naples would be one kingdom, and Prospero's family would be on the throne.

Now, as we know, Ferdinand and Miranda had fallen for one another the moment they met, and you might have thought Prospero would have left it there. After all, things couldn't have been better. Next would come the first kiss, then a melting of eyes, and that would be that. The lovers would be as good as wed.

But Prospero had other plans. He had decided to make life difficult for the young lovers, for he wanted to make sure they really did love each other. So, much to Miranda's horror, Prospero – quite out of the blue – accused Ferdinand of being a spy, who had come to the island to take it over for himself. He shouted at the horrified young man, and told him he would chain his legs together and keep him prisoner.

You should have seen Miranda's lovely face! She was astonished as she watched her father roar at her beloved Ferdinand. She couldn't understand why he wasn't as happy as she was.

Then Ferdinand, heroic to the last, raised

his sword. But as soon as he did, Prospero pointed his magic staff at him; and the young man knew better than to argue with *that*. Off he was marched by Prospero, and set to work shifting logs. Unbelievable, isn't it! But then, as you're beginning to realise, my master works in mysterious ways.

I wanted to see what happened next, but I couldn't wait around. Prospero's exile could only end when he got his dukedom back from Antonio and, for that to happen, there was going to have to be a whole lot more magic. My freedom would have to wait a little longer. This time, though, I kept my impatience well hidden, for I didn't want Prospero to remind me again that *he* was in charge. And his words:

Thou shalt be free
As mountain winds

made me do as I was told quite willingly.

Those winds of freedom blew happily through my veins as I busied myself with my next task. And, as I worked, I kept an eye on what was happening to those lovers. For I have ways and means of finding out what's going on, you know. Nothing escapes Ariel's watchful eye!

I gazed into a rock pool here, listened into a conch shell there and, in that way, I saw and heard Miranda's sighs as her beloved Ferdinand heaved those logs.

I heard her beg him to let her help, and heard him refuse. I laughed as he asked her name and then rolled 'Miranda' round and round on his tongue as if it were sugar.

I smiled as he told her he was a prince and then, remembering that his father was surely drowned, added sadly that he was probably a king. And that smile of mine grew broader as I heard Miranda ask that strange, human question, 'Do you love me?' for I knew, of course, Ferdinand's answer would be 'Yes'.

Then, finally, when that bold daughter of Prospero asked Ferdinand to marry her, I fairly whooped with joy! My love-spell was accomplished, and I could feel the mountain wind tugging me away from the sea, away from Prospero's island, towards freedom.

Once more, though, I was disappointed. It still wasn't time for me to be given my precious freedom. That tugging was Prospero, summoning me again. Oh, how insistently did my master call me on that magical afternoon! There were times when I felt I was in two places at one time, or that after my tempest, time and tide themselves stopped.

When I arrived at his cave, Prospero gave me orders to bring a host of magical spirits to him, for he wanted to put on a special play for Ferdinand and Miranda. This play was to be a 'masque' and, because kings and queens pay a great deal of money to have masques performed in their palaces, I knew it was going to be quite something. And I knew the magical spirits would be delighted, too, for nothing pleased them more than singing and dancing and wearing wonderful costumes.

I couldn't wait to get started so, faster than a wave breaks, I rounded up as many spirits as I could find. And then what a masque we showed those young lovers!

If Ferdinand and Miranda had imagined, when they first set eyes on one another, that they were seeing gods, then what Prospero and I conjured up showed them the real thing. It was magnificence itself – a truly spectacular affair. And its purpose wasn't just to entertain them. It was also a blessing on their lives together.

First came Iris, the goddess of the rainbow, and she was a sight to behold with her glittering, arched bow of colours and her saffron wings. She summoned Ceres, the goddess of the harvest, and then none other than Juno, the great goddess of light. Together, the three goddesses blessed Ferdinand and Miranda and wished them joy and prosperity and children – all the gifts Nature could bring them.

Ferdinand was enraptured! But we hadn't finished – for remember, I had an entire cast of spirits with me. Soon nymphs, and reapers, and (of course!) music surrounded Ferdinand

and his bride-to-be. Sound and song filled the air; and joy, happiness, and goodness filled every heart. In those golden moments, this island really seemed like Paradise.

Until Prospero spoke.

Now, as you can imagine, in twelve years I have seen my master in many a rage; but never have I seen him so angry, and neither had Miranda. Trembling with fury, he roared at my poor spirits. He told them to stop their dancing, and he ordered them to leave immediately. They did, though they didn't know why they had to go and were not at all pleased. Everyone was mystified and disappointed, for there seemed no reason to stop the masque. And there *was* no outward reason. The reason was *inside* Prospero. His mind was suddenly on darker things.

Prospero, you see, had another slave, and that was Sycorax's son, Caliban. And Caliban, as you'd expect of someone with a witch for a mother and the Devil for a father, was not at all trustworthy! Nothing happened on this island without Prospero getting to know about it, and on that day he'd realised Caliban was up to no good. The magnificence of the masque had enchanted him, but all the while he'd known that Caliban had met two other survivors of our tempest – a couple of clowns by the names of Stephano and Trinculo – and between them they had hatched a terrible plot. A murder plot, in fact!

Prospero knew he couldn't put it off any longer – he had to act, for his life was in danger. Reality had to be faced, so the masque had to stop and its actors and props and scenery had to be sent away. The masque had seemed like Paradise but, sadly, Paradise isn't real.

Our revels now are ended. These our actors,
As I foretold you, were all spirits and
Are melted into air, into thin air

was what Prospero said and, as he turned away from the happy, young lovers and went off to think his sad, dark thoughts, he added:

We are such stuff
As dreams are made on, and our little life
Is rounded in a sleep.

I'm going to let you into a secret now. I wasn't going to tell you because, as I've said more than once, we airy spirits don't weep, or feel pity, or love. Airy spirits fly away from all those human emotions, don't we? Or *do* we?

My secret is that, before the masque began, I asked Prospero if he loved me. Yes! Amazing though that sounds, I did. Me – a spirit, whose emotions are all air! And do you know how he answered? He said, *Dearly, my delicate Ariel.*

Now, I ask you – *why* did I want to know that? I don't 'do' love, do I?

I can only leave you to guess at the answer. Perhaps it was simply because 'love' was in the air. Perhaps it was because I knew Prospero was going to give me my liberty and that meant we would soon part for ever. Or perhaps it was because I knew Prospero was right in what he said. I *am* 'such stuff as dreams are made on'.

And if I am, well – dreams are lost if there's no one to dream them, aren't they?

Act Three

I warned you our story would be all about love, and adventure, and magic, and murder plots. Yes, murder *plots* – for there were two of those – two wicked plots that transformed this beautiful, peaceful island into a place of violent and murderous thoughts.

One, as you already know, was hatched by Caliban and his new-found friends. You'll hear all about that soon! The other, which was hatched against King Alonso, is the one

I'll tell you about first. So, let me take you to the shore where King Alonso, his brother Sebastian, and Prospero's brother Antonio were shipwrecked, along with Gonzalo and two courtiers called Adrian and Francisco.

Now, as soon as you hear the name Antonio, you'll probably guess who was behind this piece of wickedness. For hadn't Antonio as good as murdered his own brother, Prospero, and his innocent child? And if you consider *why* Antonio had stooped so low – because he was consumed with greed and the lust for power – that will give you a clue to his motives.

For he was *still* greedy and ambitious, and would stop at nothing to achieve his goal. This time, though, his ambition wasn't for himself, but for his old friend Sebastian. He wanted him to become King of Naples. But, make no mistake, Antonio wasn't just thinking of *Sebastian's* welfare! Oh no – he knew *he* would benefit, too! After all, if you can't be king yourself, isn't being the king's close friend the next best thing?

So now let's have a good look at those men – for they're certainly worth looking at! They're the richest and most important men in Italy, and they're quite a sight to see in their fine wedding clothes. Let me help you picture them.

First, down there on the sand, is King Alonso. He's richly dressed but, oh, he doesn't look much like a great king any more. He's been driven half-mad with grief, and who can blame him? He's just said goodbye to his daughter Claribel, who's married an African king, so there's little chance he'll see her again. And now, to crown it all, he thinks his dear son Ferdinand – his pride and joy and heir to his throne – is drowned. No wonder he's in no mood to listen to good old Gonzalo.

Gonzalo is gazing round at the island in wonder and, as always, he sees everything that's good about it. That's what Gonzalo's like – he looks on the bright side of things. No wonder my master loved him. He just can't get over how bright and fresh their clothes are, after all they've been through.

It's as though the sea has actually *improved* them, he says. How clever of him to notice my sea-change! No one else did.

I must say, he's got quite an imagination, this old man. Now he's imagining himself as king of the island, and getting quite carried away at the thought of it. What a true Paradise it could be, with King Gonzalo in charge. There would be no need for laws because everyone would be free to live exactly as they wanted; there would be no machines, no money, no work. Everyone would be equal and live in harmony with Nature. It would be idyllic!

And all this time, while Gonzalo's weaving his little fantasies, Antonio and Sebastian are poking fun at him. They're like a couple of schoolboys, making a fool of him every time he opens his mouth. They're enjoying having a laugh at the old man's expense, and maybe it seems like good, clean fun. But don't be fooled. There's something sinister about that boyish laughter. Those two may sound good-natured, but underneath their smiles, they're capable of the most profound evil, as you're about to see. For now I play my music, and as my magic melody floats towards them on the sea-breeze, they breathe in its enchantment...

As soon as King Alonso, Gonzalo, and the courtiers hear the first notes, they're overcome by drowsiness. Gonzalo and the courtiers give in to my sleepy magic at once, but Alonso – though he would love to escape from his sad thoughts – is afraid to sleep. He is a king, after all, and responsible for all his subjects. Who knows what dangers lurk in this strange land?

Little does King Alonso know that the greatest danger of all is right under his royal nose! His friend and ally Antonio and his own brother Sebastian are not what they seem. Just listen to how that cunning snake Antonio slyly offers to protect his king:

We two, my lord
Will guard your person while you take your rest
And watch your safety.

Don't be like King Alonso! Don't trust Antonio's words for a second! There he is, that too-trusting king, curled up beside Gonzalo, fast asleep and at peace at last. Now listen again to Antonio. Listen, and you'll hear what a clever persuader he is.

See how slowly, slowly his smooth words, like water dripping onto a rock, wear down his friend Sebastian as he persuades him to enter into a murder plot. I think you'll agree that although it's evil, it's *brilliant*. First of all, hear how he gets Sebastian's attention and turns his thoughts to murder:

My strong imagination sees a crown
Dropping upon thy head.

Clever, isn't he? Sebastian can hardly believe what he's hearing. He thinks he must be having some weird, waking dream. But you can be sure he knows what Antonio's hinting at. You can be sure that *he's* imagining a crown on his head, too.

Now Antonio puts the next bit of his plan

into action. He begins to talk about Ferdinand – remember, he's the *true* heir to the throne – and he tells Sebastian there's no hope that Ferdinand's still alive.

'Tis as impossible that he's undrowned
As he that sleeps here, swims

he says.

Then the crafty fox goes on to talk about Ferdinand's sister Claribel – because if he's dead, she's the next in line to the throne. Listen as he tells Sebastian how far away she is. Oh how shamelessly he exaggerates! It's true that Claribel is far away in Tunisia, but Antonio says she's *so* far away that the journey would take as long as it takes a baby to grow into a man!

See the spark of interest in Sebastian's eyes? How it glints and grows. His breath's coming faster as he listens and begins to realise that these dreams could become a reality. After all, when it comes to getting rid of relations who stand in the way of your ambition, no one is a bigger expert than Antonio. He's done it all before *and* reaped the rewards!

However, there's one question Sebastian has to ask, and it's a question any decent person would:

But for your conscience?

For just a few moments, King Alonso is safe; for Sebastian's question means he could never live with himself if he murdered his own brother. But Antonio's too clever to admit to feeling any guilt. His face is a picture of scorn, and he doesn't take long to answer. He doesn't need to wonder whether his conscience bothers him. Of course it doesn't!

If my conscience was a blister on my toe, he tells Sebastian. *I'd just put on slippers*!

And with that problem out of the way, Antonio's hand is twitching to draw his sword and do the deed. Any minute now, he knows, the sleepers could wake up. Listen carefully, for here comes his masterstroke:

He offers to do the killing! How clever is *that*? He tells Sebastian that all *he* has to do is get rid of the feeble old Gonzalo. It would, of course, be too risky to let him live for, unlike the others, he'd be sure to want justice done.

Now what do you think? Don't you almost *admire* Antonio? What a wicked genius he is, for the one thing that might change Sebastian's mind would be the thought of doing the deed. After all, killing your own brother is a terrible thing to do, no matter what the rewards, if you have a conscience.

That was when I intervened, for at that moment the would-be murderers raised their swords and prepared to strike. Invisible as the air, I floated close to Gonzalo, and sang my song into his ear:

> *While you here do snoring lie,*
> *Open-eyed conspiracy*
> *His time doth take.*
> *If of life you keep a care,*
> *Shake off slumber and beware.*
> *Awake, awake!*

Softly and gently, my music weaved its magic around his dreams, alerting him to danger, and waking him.

I had to wake Gonzalo, of course. Prospero would never, ever have let his old friend be harmed. And when I did, I can tell you all hell broke loose! The moment Gonzalo opened his eyes and saw Antonio and Sebastian with their swords drawn, he cried out and shook the king awake. (That kind old man would think of the king's safety before his own.)

For a moment Antonio and Sebastian must have thought they'd been found out. But you won't be surprised to hear that they managed to worm their way out of trouble. Looking as innocent as new-born babies, they said they'd heard a dreadful bellowing and, thinking bulls or lions were coming, had bravely rushed to defend the sleeping king. What a devious trickster Antonio was, and how willing Sebastian was to be led astray. And those villains got away with it, too.

No sooner had King Alonso woken, than his thoughts turned back to Ferdinand; he was anxious to move away from danger and look for him. He was almost sure it would be a pointless search, but there was still a tiny glimmer of hope inside his heart.

And there, for the time being, we'll leave him; for now I'm going to tell you about the second murder plot: the plot against Prospero, hatched by Caliban and his two new friends. But, before I do, I must introduce you properly to Caliban. He's a strange character and an important one, so you should know him well.

How can I describe him? Well, let's say that if you saw Caliban's twisted tree-root of a body and his big, clawed feet, I'm sure you'd think you'd seen a monster. And I daresay if you *smelt* him, you'd think he was monstrously smelly. Certainly, he's a rough, earthy fellow with no airs and graces and – some would say – little in the way of finer feelings. Yet, even now, I often find myself wondering how he is and what he's doing.

Caliban, you see, could be considered lord of this isle. It had, after all, belonged to his mother, Sycorax, before she died. And, for all his roughness, perhaps Caliban really is the best ruler it could have. He understands it, you see. From the time he could crawl, he knew where to find the best berries, and the tastiest salt, and the sweetest water; and when Prospero and Miranda arrived and took charge, he happily shared all his knowledge with them. Surprisingly, at first, Caliban didn't mind doing all their tough, dirty work; and when Prospero and Miranda started to teach him how to speak their language, he was a willing pupil.

It came to a dreadful end though, when Miranda grew into a beautiful young girl. You see, Caliban had the idea that he, as king of the island, should have her as his queen. And one look at Caliban makes it clear that this was not a choice Miranda or her father was going to make. Miranda, after all, is a beauty; and Caliban – for better or for worse – is a beast.

Once Prospero realised what Caliban wanted – a wife and family – he was both shocked and furious. He was afraid for his daughter's safety, too, and so he shut Caliban up in a cave and only allowed him out to work. He treated him like an animal and, in return, Caliban acted like one.

Beast though Caliban was, I believe he *did* want to learn. He remembered things he'd been taught by Prospero and Miranda, you see – like the names of the stars, and the story of the man in the moon. Perhaps, if Prospero had given him more time, Caliban would have learned and understood much more. Perhaps, if things had been different, he could have sung my songs – for he always loved my music. But Caliban didn't learn enough. Here's what he said about the 'language' Prospero and Miranda had tried so hard to teach him:

You taught me language, and my profit on't
Is, I know how to curse.

Oh yes – I'll say that for Caliban – he was mighty good at cursing! And on the afternoon of our story, when the tempest was over but the sky was still grey, he was in as foul a mood as ever he had been. How he cursed Prospero! This is what he said:

All the infections that the sun sucks up
From bogs, fens, flats, on Prospero fall, and make him
By inch-meal a disease. His spirits hear me,
And yet I needs must curse.

Dreadful, isn't it? If Caliban had had the power, he'd surely have infected our master with the worst diseases he could conjure up. For Caliban was always angry that he was kept prisoner by Prospero and treated so badly by him.

Although Caliban and I were both Prospero's slaves, you see, our lives couldn't have been more different. *My* work was all magic, enchantments, music and wild flights of fancy, whereas Caliban's was just hard labour – gathering logs, mostly, to keep Prospero's cave cosy. It was hardly the kind of work you could be *inspired* by and, oh, he did it so unwillingly! He grudged Prospero every splinter of that firewood, and it's easy to see why. For Caliban was king of the isle, wasn't he? So when you look at it like that – a king being made into a slave by a man who's taken over his kingdom – is it any wonder Caliban was furious? Is it any wonder he did his work slowly and with as many foul curses as he possibly could? And, believe me, every time he cursed, or refused to do what he was told, he was horribly punished.

Prospero had to punish Caliban, for he had no reward of freedom with which to bribe him, as he had with me. Caliban could only have his freedom if Prospero left the island. Or if Prospero died...

Which brings us to the second murder plot, which Caliban hatched against Prospero and which – be warned – was monstrously brutal, monstrously vicious and, above all, monstrously stupid.

Now, to set the scene, I provided a most dramatic sound effect. Imagine hearing Caliban's curse, roared in as furious a voice as you've ever heard, followed by an ear-splitting *crack* of thunder. How splendidly loud were my booms! Mercilessly, I rumbled down on the poor, angry monster, as he trudged along with his load of logs, growling and grumbling all the while. And, of course, my thunder made Caliban's foul mood a hundred times fouler! He just couldn't help letting out a string of curses.

He knew, of course, he'd be punished later because, even if Prospero wasn't within earshot, there were always spirits hiding under stones, beneath leaves, within flowers. They'd tell Prospero, for sure, and then the punishments would come as surely as rainbows follow sun-showers!

Unfair, wasn't it? Think what it must have been like to be Caliban...

You do something wrong one day, and that night you're pinched all over with sharp pains so you can't sleep. Next day, you're so exhausted you work too slowly, and this time you're pushed into a muddy swamp.

And those little spirits that Prospero keeps all over the island could change their shapes like me (though not as expertly). So your next punishment could be a great crowd of apes pulling horrible faces, chattering at the tops of their voices, and then biting you.

Or, if you think *that's* bad, how do you fancy having hedgehogs appear under your bare feet as you're dragging your firewood along, and driving their spikes into your soles?

Or being wound all round by adders that squeeze you tight, and then sway to and fro in front of your face, flicking their tongues in and out, and hissing into your ears till you feel you'll go mad?

It was certainly no fun being Caliban.

Let's take a closer look: here he is, cursing fit to burst and then dreading the consequences, and here am I, thundering down on him. And then, just as he thinks the day can't get any worse, the most hideous spirit he has ever seen appears.

Now this spirit's a bit odd... He walks on two legs, or rather he sways from side to side – for he's been shipwrecked and hasn't quite found his land-legs yet. He wears a red-and-yellow suit and a red-and-yellow hat with three points, and to each point there's a little bell attached. He's scared out of his wits and, because he's just escaped from the sea, he doesn't want another drenching. So he's eyeing the black cloud overhead and thinking miserably that it reminds him of a big barrel of wine, just about to pour its contents on top of his silly head.

Yes, I'm sure you've guessed – it's not a spirit at all. It's the first of those two clowns I told you about. It's Trinculo, King Alonso's jester, washed up from the shipwreck. He hasn't a clue where he is, and he could certainly do with a drink to calm his frayed nerves!

And this is where the comedy begins, for Caliban, terrified by the sight of the 'spirit', has crawled under a piece of old sheeting that's lying washed up on the beach, and now Trinculo sees him. Or rather he sees a large, smelly cloak with a pair of large, smelly clawed feet sticking out from under it, and he decides to investigate. When he does; he sees he's made quite a discovery!

Look how excited Trinculo is. He's found a monster – half-man, half-fish. What a find! See how his greedy eyes sparkle, for no sooner has he decided that's what Caliban is than he's planning how much money he can make out of him. What a rogue that jester is. He's rubbing his hands together with glee as he imagines how much people back home will pay to see this freak. It's better than a bearded lady, or a giant, or a baby with two heads. He'll make his fortune.

Of course *I* know what he's up to and *I'm* going to make life difficult for him – so what do I do? I thunder again! And, just as I'd hoped, Trinculo, who doesn't want another soaking, crawls under Caliban's cloak. Imagine it! One large, fishy-smelling cloak with one pair of large, smelly Caliban-feet sticking out one end, and one pair of small, red-and-yellow Trinculo-feet sticking out the other. The stage is set for the entry of the second clown, and what a clown *he* is.

Enter Stephano, King Alonso's butler – and be warned, he is *very* much the worse for drink, for he's floated ashore astride a barrel of wine, which he's now proceeding to empty! He's taking great swigs from the wooden bottle, and he's singing very loudly and very tunelessly, and when Caliban hears him, he's beside himself with terror. The first 'spirit', he thinks, has been joined by another. He peeps out from under the cloak and, before he knows what's happening, he's being offered a drink by Stephano. Caliban has never tasted alcohol, and at first he spits it out, but Stephano doesn't give up. He tells him to 'open his chops', and this time he pours the drink down Caliban's throat.

Meanwhile, under the cloak, Trinculo's puzzled. He hears Stephano's voice – but surely his old friend and drinking companion is drowned? Like Caliban, he begins to think *he's* being haunted by spirits, and cries out. And when Stephano hears Trinculo's voice, he can't believe his luck!

Four legs and two voices, he says. *A most delicate monster!*

Eventually, those two bits of flotsam realise what's happening. Stephano drags Trinculo out from under the cloak and you can imagine how relieved and delighted they are to find they've both survived the storm. Look at them dance around!

Do you remember what Ferdinand thought when he first saw Miranda? And what Miranda thought when she first saw Ferdinand? They both thought they were seeing gods, for I had made sure they were completely blinded by love. Well, there was certainly magic in the island's air that afternoon, for here's what Caliban said when he saw the drunken old butler Stephano:

That's a brave god, and bears celestial liquor. I will kneel to him.

And that's where the second murder plot began to take shape. For Caliban was entranced by a very ordinary mortal (or rather, he was entranced by the effects of a very ordinary mortal's very ordinary wine), and he suddenly realised he'd found his heart's desire. Or *thought* he had.

Listen to what he's saying to Stephano now:

I'll show thee the best springs; I'll pluck thee berries;
I'll fish for thee, and get thee wood enough.
A plague upon the tyrant that I serve!
I'll bear him no more sticks, but follow thee,
Thou wondrous man.

Ridiculous, isn't it? A few mouthfuls of wine, and there's Caliban swearing to follow this man for the rest of his days. And of course Stephano's lapping it up like a cat does cream. He's never felt so important in his life. Suddenly he – a mere servant – is being treated like royalty! Even Trinculo sees it's ridiculous. As you might guess, he's really put out, for he's jealous of Stephano's new friend, and so he heaps insult upon insult on Caliban.

But things are starting to become dangerous now. Stephano's suddenly got ideas well above his station. He's drunk with wine, for sure – but he's also drunk with power. King Alonso's drowned, isn't he? And his son, and all the courtiers? Aren't he and Trinculo the sole survivors of the storm? Doesn't that make them lords of the island?

Meanwhile Caliban, his head spinning, is happier than he's ever been. He's got a new master, and *this* master won't punish him like Prospero. *This* master is going to be a great master. Caliban will do anything for him – in exchange for a drink.

Watch them stagger along the beach together. Aren't they a laughable trio, if ever there was one. With Stephano and Trinculo as lords of the island, what hope has the place got? But now, as they weave their way along, the comedy's starting to fade, and things are becoming sinister. That dark mind of Caliban's is growing darker and darker. The resentment he's been feeling during all those years of imprisonment is coming to the surface. He's got a fine new master, and now he's going to make sure he keeps him – by getting rid of the old one, for ever…

Trinculo, Stephano and Caliban staggered along the sands, and all the while Stephano, who was even drunker than his friend, was making his plans. He and Trinculo were going to rule the island, with Caliban as their servant. Oh, how ridiculous I found them. For of course I was with them, every staggering step of the way. And, believe me, I had my fun with those clowns!

Have you ever wondered what it would be like to be invisible? Have you ever thought about what you could *do*? Because it's great to be a storm at sea, or a thunderbolt, or a lightning flash – all these things give you enormous power. But to be invisible ... now *that* is perhaps the most powerful magic of all, and the most fun. Listen to what it's like...

When you're invisible, you can be as close to people as the hairs on their heads, are to their scalps. You can hear them breathe, and whisper, and sigh. You can almost hear their thoughts, yet they haven't the slightest idea you're there.

Now that's what I call 'power' – because you can make such fools of them, and I used my cloak of invisibility to make even bigger fools of Stephano and Trinculo than they already were. As you hear how I did it, I'm sure you're going to wish *you* had a cloak of invisibility like me.

There they were, Stephano and Trinculo, on the sands, so drunk I'll swear they would have punched the air if it had dared blow in their faces. And there was Caliban, fawning at Stephano's feet and swearing to follow him all his days. Oh how shamelessly he flattered that silly old butler!

Now, the more Caliban flattered Stephano, and the more puffed-up with pride Stephano became, the angrier it made Trinculo. For Trinculo, drunk as he was, was not as foolish as his friend, and he could see how stupid Stephano's plans to rule the island really were. He knew how ridiculous Stephano was to trust Caliban, too.

And as they went on in the direction of Prospero's cave, arguing about Caliban, *I* kept close, weaving my way in and out of the air, breathing in every word these fools uttered, and waiting for the opportunity to play my tricks. I knew, you see, that I had to split up those two silly friends. For Caliban could only persuade *Stephano* to plot with him against Prospero. Trinculo would never, ever be convinced.

Soon my chance came. When Caliban told Stephano he would only serve *him*, and that Trinculo was not 'valiant' enough to be his master, Trinculo's blood fairly boiled.

Thou liest! he shouted at Caliban. Then he hurled insult after insult at him, which made Caliban turn to his new 'master' for protection. Would you believe it, he asked Stephano to bite Trinculo to death! And Stephano didn't let him down – he told Trinculo to keep a good tongue in his head, and warned him that if he didn't behave, he'd be *hanged*!

It really was funny to watch, but I knew I had no time to be entertained. I seized my chance to split up those clowns, and let the murder plot develop. As Caliban told Stephano how badly Prospero treated him, I shouted, *Thou liest!* I shouted it in a voice that sounded a bit like Trinculo's, and my trick worked a treat. Caliban was furious with Trinculo, and *so was Stephano*. This time, he threatened to knock his teeth out if he said one more nasty thing.

Poor old Trinculo, he didn't have a clue why he was being picked on. He protested his innocence, but Stephano only had ears for Caliban. He wanted to hear all about his plans to get rid of Prospero. And the more Caliban told him, the more tempted he was by the thought of being lord of the island.

Remember the first murder plot? The one against King Alonso? Antonio did the same thing, didn't he? He tempted Sebastian by saying he could imagine him with a crown on his head, and then it wasn't long before Sebastian's thoughts turned to murder.

It was just like that with Stephano. The more Caliban spoke, the more interested he became, and when Caliban said:

I'll yield him thee asleep
Where thou mayst knock a nail into his head

that old drunkard didn't bat an eyelid at the thought of the crime he was agreeing to.

I did, though. I called out again – *Thou liest, thou canst not!*

This time, Caliban almost hit Trinculo. Both he and Stephano were furious; but as for me – if I'd had sides, they would have split with laughter. I knew I was almost there, so I said, *Thou liest!* one last time. And, to my delight, Stephano took a swipe at Trinculo. Then Trinculo, who still hadn't a clue what was going on, very nearly burst into tears.

What children these men were. But I suppose *I* was like a child, too, with my naughty tricks!

Those tricks worked a treat, though. Stephano ordered Trinculo to go away, and Trinculo retreated, leaving Stephano alone for Caliban to tell him all the details of his devilish plot. And 'devilish' it certainly was. I hope you've got a strong stomach, for I'm going to tell you all the ways Caliban suggested Stephano might kill Prospero...

If he didn't fancy the first suggestion – knocking a nail into his head – he could batter Prospero's skull with a log. If *that* wasn't violent enough, he could stab him in the stomach with a stake. Or, if he preferred something a little more gory, he could cut his throat with a knife. Well, Prospero always said Caliban was a 'born devil'!

But there was something else that Caliban

told Stephano to do, and it was so important that he told him three times – *first seize his books*. For Caliban was no fool. He knew very well that without his magic books, Prospero was a weak, old man, and without the help of all us spirits, he'd be an easy victim.

Then, last of all, to make quite sure Stephano would agree to the murder, Caliban told him about Miranda. That settled it. No sooner had Caliban told the old fool how beautiful Miranda was, and what a perfect wife she'd make, than Stephano was completely hooked. If he'd had any last qualms about bludgeoning a helpless old man to death – which I don't think he had – they vanished into thin air.

Monster, he said, *I will kill this man*.

Now, as soon as Stephano had decided he'd do what Caliban wanted, he was delighted with himself! He called Trinculo back, and promised that he and Caliban would be his deputies, once he was king of the island. Then he apologised for hitting him, and Trinculo – whose head must have been well and truly spinning – said he thought it was an excellent idea, and shook his friend's hand.

Caliban, of course, was delighted. He wanted to celebrate, so he asked Stephano and Trinculo to sing him the song they'd taught him earlier.

They obliged, of course – and what a noise they made! Neither of them had a clue about music, and Caliban knew that. *That's not the tune*, he complained; and as soon as his words were out, I was there, bang on cue, with my drum and my pipe, playing the proper melody round and round the bewildered heads of those two clowns.

You should have seen Stephano and Trinculo then! Of course, they couldn't see me. All they heard was music, coming from the air, or the sand, or the sea. And they were terrified. When Caliban saw how scared they were, this is what he said:

Be not afeard, the isle is full of noises,
Sounds, and sweet airs, that give delight and

hurt not.

Sometimes a thousand twangling instruments
Will hum about mine ears; and sometimes voices,
That if I then had waked after long sleep,
Will make me sleep again; and then in dreaming,
The clouds methought would open, and show riches
Ready to drop upon me, that when I waked
I cried to dream again.

Now, I ask you – could a monster, whose every second breath is a curse, have said these words? Could a 'born devil' delight in music? Could a savage murderer dream such rich dreams that when he woke, he wept? Yet those were Caliban's words and, I'll admit to you, if I had a heart, those words would have melted it.

But I don't – and I was in the mood for more fun. So off I flew, still playing my music, in the direction of Prospero's cave. I knew Stephano and Trinculo and their 'slave' couldn't help but follow like calves, and what a merry dance I led them! Through prickly briars we went, and gorse and thorn bushes, till their legs were ripped raw. Then, when they could go no further, I dumped them in the smelliest, slimiest, most scum-covered pond I could find. And there I abandoned them as I flew off to tell the whole story to my master.

When I told Prospero what I'd done, he was pleased with me, and when he told me the next thing he'd planned for the mischief makers, I was delighted. For the last part of Prospero's punishment was the best of all. It showed, you see, which of those three foolish rogues were the *real* fools...

Prospero had, in his cave, a load of rich-looking clothes and jewellery, and he told me to fetch them. Then he and I, both invisible, held a line between us, and I hung the sparkling bits of gaudy rubbish on it, and when Caliban, Stephano and Trinculo appeared, they ran slap-bang into our glittering trap.

Stephano and Trinculo, who had convinced themselves by this time that they really were rulers of the isle, fell upon our bait with delight. They put on the bright gowns, and the gilded crowns, and every bit of silliness they could lay their greedy hands on, and they thought these bits of nonsense made them look like real noblemen.

Caliban, however, wasn't fooled. Remember, he'd seen the clouds open and show true riches, and had wept when these riches were taken away from him. Caliban knew what real beauty and quality were. He saw our bait as the worthless trash it was, and told Stephano and Trinculo to leave it. But, of course, those buffoons didn't listen to him. They went their own sweet, foolish way and loaded Caliban with as many silly garments as he could carry; and it was then, when the three of them could hardly move under the weight of their worthless 'treasure', that Prospero and I sent them well and truly running for their lives.

It was almost as much fun as the tempest! We made a whole gang of spirits change into

70

great hunting dogs, which chased our would-be murderers. How we shouted at the tops of our voices to egg those dogs on! It was as thrilling a hunt as ever I've seen, and our victims didn't stand a chance.

'Tell my goblins to give them cramps in every muscle,' Prospero said, when we'd chased them to exhaustion, 'and to pinch them so hard they'll look like spotty leopards!'

And that was, for the moment, the end of Prospero's punishment for Caliban and his friends. Now it was time for him to turn his attentions back to the real purpose of the tempest – his revenge on those royal villains King Alonso, Antonio and Sebastian.

Do you remember how Antonio and Sebastian had tried to kill Alonso and Gonzalo so that Sebastian could become King of Naples? And do you remember how I'd stopped them just as they raised their swords to strike? Well, you won't be surprised when I tell you that didn't put them off. They'd failed once, and almost been found out, but those evil men didn't forget about their plot. Not a bit. As they walked along the beach, they thought of nothing else. In fact, Antonio and Sebastian were so heartless, that when they all stopped to rest and King Alonso said he had finally given up any hope of finding his son Ferdinand alive, they were *glad*. For they knew that his grief would make him careless. That night, for sure, they would kill him.

Imagine, then, their astonishment when suddenly, out of nowhere, they heard strange, solemn, beautiful music, followed by the arrival of a host of weird and wonderful creatures! The strange beings were carrying a table, which was set with the most magnificent banquet they'd ever seen. The royal men simply couldn't believe their eyes, and the sight before them was so fantastic that they felt as if they were losing their senses. Just like my master's masque, it was all too beautiful to take in. It was too much like Paradise.

Now, along with the strange creatures (my 'gang' again) and the fabulous food, there was something else there that no one could see. Some*one*, I should say – for this time Prospero made a personal 'appearance', though he was careful to stay invisible. He had to be there, you see, for a very, very important piece of magic was about to happen. And it was the magic that, finally, made King Alonso change for good.

There they all were, those royal men, rubbing their eyes and staring at the delicious food, wondering whether they dared eat it. Everyone was tempted to try some, except Alonso. He was as cautious as ever, but eventually he was persuaded. He had, after all, nothing to lose. He felt as if his life couldn't get any worse. How wrong he was! For it was time for *my* big entrance – and this time, I wasn't a storm, or a lightning flash, or a thunder crack, and I wasn't invisible, either. Believe me, I was even *more* awesome...

Have you ever heard of a Harpy? It's quite a monster! It's got the head and upper body of a woman, and the tail, wings and claws of a massive bird. And, knowing your Ariel as you do, you'll know that when *I* appeared as a Harpy, it was the most terrifying one you could possibly imagine. That wasn't all. I summoned up a mighty flash of lightning and a deafening crack of thunder, too, so when I swooped down to strike the table with my wings, they glowed fiery gold. And as soon as they touched that table, it disappeared, and with it all the fine food. Everything vanished in the twinkling of an eye, just like the masque had done.

Once again, Paradise hadn't been real after all.

Then, when my audience thought they were going completely mad, I made my most important speech. This is how it began:

You are three men of sin, whom Destiny –
That hath to instrument this lower world,
And what is in't – the never-surfeited sea
Hath caused to belch up you. And on this island,
Where man doth not inhabit – you 'mongst men

Being most unfit to live – I have made you mad.

Oh, how these words cut through Alonso, Antonio and Sebastian. They pierced them as deeply as if they had been their own murderous swords; for the truth hurts. If they had any pride left (and I think by this time Alonso had precious little), that pride took a terrible tumble. It was, I'm sure you'll agree, a far better revenge than mere drowning!

I couldn't have been more insulting, could I? For didn't I describe them as vomit, and tell them they weren't worthy of being alive? Strong words from an airy spirit! I wasn't finished, either. I went on to list all their sins. I faced them fairly and squarely with all the evil deeds they'd done, and I left them in no doubt whatsoever that the tempest and shipwreck were a punishment for all their past evil. In particular, I pointed out to Alonso that the mighty powers that had made the tempest had taken his son away from him.

Now, of course, that didn't mean that Ferdinand had been drowned, as we know – but Alonso thought it did. If any hope remained that his son had survived the storm, I washed those last traces clean away.

Oh how those three men shook with fear and shame! My words were like a great mirror held up in front of them, which forced them to see themselves, and their crimes, for the first time.

What did Alonso's fine clothes matter now, or his position as King of Naples? He saw himself as never before – a flawed man who'd lost his son because of his sins. Hadn't he as good as killed Ferdinand himself? And didn't he deserve to die for his deed? How dreadfully guilty and grief-stricken that man felt. I can tell you, he'd have preferred to be dead!

But my master's purpose wasn't simply to show these men the error of their ways. It wasn't an empty revenge. That would have been pointless – for I've told you before that Prospero's magic spells are always spun for good, even though they may seem cruel.

Sometimes you have to be cruel to be kind, and so, at the end of my tirade, I told King Alonso that the only way he could avoid a dreadful life from that day onwards was to truly repent. And then, with one last glorious thunderclap, I left.

I didn't have to wait to hear Alonso's response. I knew he *would* repent, for he was a broken man. Antonio and Sebastian may have drawn their swords at the sight of my Harpy, but the king didn't. He had reached the end; all the fight had left him. And, you know, I believe he was genuinely sorry. He had experienced such loss, such grief, that afternoon. Now at last he understood how his actions had made Prospero suffer.

Yes, King Alonso was at his wits' end with grief. This is what he said:

> *O, it is monstrous: monstrous!*
> *Methought the billows spoke and told me of it,*
> *The winds did sing to me, and the thunder,*
> *That deep and dreadful organ-pipe, pronounced*
> *The name of Prospero.*

He was right, too. The sea and the winds and the thunder *had* spoken to him; for am I not all these things? Am I not the voice of the elements, the voice of nature? And, as I've told you so many times, I don't have the feelings of humans... *I* don't feel pity, do I?

Of course I don't. Does the wind feel pity for the leaves it blows from the trees? Or the lightning feel pity for the branches it splits in two? But, you know, the story of *The Tempest* is a story of magical changes. Didn't I tell you, right at the beginning, that *no one* was the same after that day? Well, perhaps that includes me. Perhaps the magic of that day affected me, too. For when I heard King Alonso say that he would search for his drowned son, and lie deep down on the ocean bed with him, I felt something that I'd never felt before.

It wasn't much. Just a tiny feeling for that man's grief, that was all. But if I, who's made of air, felt a grain of pity for King Alonso, you may be sure that my noble master pitied him much, much more. And, as you're about to find out, that pity moved his heart to forgiveness.

Where the bee sucks there suck I;
In a cowslip's bell I lie;
There I couch when owls do fly,
After summer merrily.
Merrily, merrily, shall I live now,
Under the blossom that hangs on the bough.

That was the last song I sang as Prospero's slave, and what a joyful song it was. For it was, truly, my freedom-song, and oh, I was merry when I sang it!

Have you ever stood at the sea's edge, where its waters break upon the shore, and heard the steady music of the waves lapping around your feet? Next time you do, listen well and, perhaps, underneath the water's hum, you'll hear the soft beating of Ariel's heart.

Or walk in the woods where the songbirds sing, and perhaps you'll hear my laughter drowning out the blackbirds' sweet melodies.

Or sit among the wild grasses, surrounded by flowers, with drowsy bumblebees droning round your head. Perhaps you'll hear me singing that freedom-song of mine again. But be warned – you'll have to listen very well if you want to make out my words!

It was after six o'clock when I sang my song, and Prospero had promised to give me my freedom by then. Six o'clock came and went, however, and still there was more magic to do. But I didn't complain. My airy heart was as light as a gnat's wing; my whole being was sheer happiness, for I knew that soon I *would* be free.

Imagine that, after a lifetime of slavery.

Imagine being able to come and go as you please, after years and years of being sent and summoned.

Imagine having all the time in the world.

So as I flew off to fetch King Alonso and his companions and bring them to Prospero, I was charged with excitement. The very air around me crackled and hissed as though there was a lightning-storm!

And, as I flew, a part of me was listening to Prospero, for the words he spoke were so important that they chased behind me on the wind. He didn't know I was listening, for he was talking to himself. But I heard him all right, as he spoke of all the magic he had made in the past twelve years – of how he had darkened the sun, and made the winds blow, and summoned up great storms; of how his power had split trees, and uprooted them; of how he had even made the dead live again. And I wondered at the mix of emotions he must be feeling as he spoke.

Then, at last, he said the words I had

longed to hear for twelve long years. And oh, how my airy heart raced when I heard them:

But this rough magic
I here abjure. And when I have required
Some heavenly music – which even now I do –
To work mine end upon their senses that
This airy charm is for, I'll break my staff,
Bury it certain fathoms in the earth,
And deeper than did ever plummet sound
I'll drown my book.

At long, long last he'd break and bury that magic staff and throw that magic book into the sea; at last he'd take off his magic cloak and wear the sober clothes of a duke. At last I'd be free – but not quite yet.

There was one, final, all-important piece of work to be done, and for it Prospero needed his 'heavenly music'. And who could the musician be but Ariel! As my master drew a circle in the sand, I played my most enchanting melody which, like a strong medicine, had the power to calm the madness of all who heard it.

For Alonso, Antonio and Sebastian had been quite mad ever since I appeared to them as the Harpy and forced them to see their sins. I'd driven them frantic with guilt, just as my master wanted me to.

You should have seen how they threw themselves around! Poor Gonzalo did his best to comfort his king, and the courtiers Adrian and Francisco tried to calm Antonio and Sebastian, but the only thing that helped them was that music of mine – the music that can heal the deepest wound, and banish the greatest fear.

So, as my melody drew that sorry crowd nearer to Prospero's circle, their terror began to subside and, when they reached it, they stood, spell-stopped. They stared at Prospero, unable to understand what they were seeing, for it was as if their brains were boiled inside their skulls. And Prospero, still in his magic cloak and with his magic book and staff in his hands, stood silently watching them. Then, finally, he spoke.

Now, you might have expected him to vent his rage on the villains who had done him so much wrong, but he didn't. Instead, the first thing my master did was to praise Gonzalo for all his kindness, and promise to reward him. Then he turned to the 'three men of sin'.

They must have been quaking in their boots, wondering what dreadful punishment he would give them, but instead Prospero did as he'd told me he would do.

He *forgave* them.

But so strong was the magic trance they were in that even when Prospero told his brother, *I do forgive thee, unnatural though thou art*, Antonio had not the slightest idea who was forgiving him. In fact, not one of the men in that magic circle knew who this great magician, who had such control over them, really was. How could they have known – for wasn't Prospero, the former Duke of Milan, long dead? Hadn't they made sure of that, the day they'd cast him out to sea?

At long last, it was time for them to know the truth. Prospero sent me to his cave to fetch his hat and rapier – the ones he'd worn when he was Duke of Milan – and I helped him remove his magic cloak and dress himself. Then he threw his arms round King Alonso (who couldn't believe his eyes), and welcomed him to the island as naturally as if he were greeting guests at his palace in Milan. And no sooner had Alonso recognised him than he apologised sincerely for all he'd done, and humbly gave him back his dukedom.

Yes, King Alonso was genuinely sorry. There was no doubt that his suffering had made him see the error of his ways. And, of course, he still believed that Ferdinand was dead, and that he had died because of *his* sins; and, I must say, my master was in no hurry to reassure him. Oh no, he didn't rush to tell him Ferdinand had survived the tempest. There was still a little mischief left in the serious old Duke Prospero! For when Alonso spoke of the loss of his son, my master, with a very straight face, said, 'And I have lost a daughter.'

Wasn't that a bit unkind! Although it was true – Prospero *had* lost Miranda, for she'd soon be Ferdinand's wife. But he knew perfectly well that Alonso would think he meant that she'd died, and Alonso fell for his trick.

'If only,' he said sadly, 'your daughter and my son were alive and well, and were king and queen of Naples!'

How my master must have laughed inwardly as he heard those words! And how teasingly he smiled as he led King Alonso to the mouth of his cave and pointed in to where Ferdinand and Miranda were sitting, playing chess and looking lovingly into one another's eyes!

So, in the end, our story has a happy ending. Gonzalo, that good and wise old man, summed it up when he said:

In one voyage
Did Claribel her husband find at Tunis,
And Ferdinand her brother found a wife
Where he himself was lost; Prospero, his dukedom

In a poor isle, and all of us ourselves,
When no man was his own.

Listen to those last words again: 'When no man was his own'. Gonzalo was right, wasn't he? Everyone changed that afternoon, when their minds were so full of my magic that they couldn't think straight.

Ferdinand and Miranda fell in love and changed from boy and girl to future king and queen.

King Alonso changed from traitor to friend, and from grief-stricken man to proud and happy father.

Prospero changed from a great magician to a serious duke, and where Alonso gained a daughter, he gained a fine son.

Then there were the two clowns, Stephano and Trinculo, who'd wanted to rule this island and had ended up being dragged through thorns, and dumped in muddy pools, and chased by hounds. I rather think that, in days to come, they looked back and saw their whole adventure as a kind of drunken nightmare. I don't think they'll ever have ideas above their station again, though whether they changed much is anyone's guess. When I finally fetched them and delivered them to Alonso, they *said* they were sorry – but who knows how sorry they actually felt.

And what about Antonio and Sebastian? Did *they* really change? Did the hardships they suffered make them see the error of their ways and become good and noble men? Were *their* consciences pricked when they were shown their sins?

Your guess is as good as mine. All I know is that Prospero, who knew they'd tried to murder Alonso, could very easily have ruined them by telling the truth, and he chose not to. *They* knew he knew, though – so once they all got home to Italy, they'd have to think hard before they tried any more of their tricks. They'd have to at least *appear* to be good and noble men.

And that is the end of my story of *The Tempest*. After resting in Prospero's cave, the royal party boarded their ship for the journey home, and the very last piece of spriting I did was to promise them calm seas and gentle winds. Then off they sailed to plan another wedding, leaving the island to me, and to Caliban. And oh, what a wonderful sight it was to see that royal ship disappear over the horizon! What a marvellous feeling it was to be as free as the air, at long, long last!

Now, you know how *I* changed from slave to free spirit, but what about that monster Caliban? Did *he* change, when he got his freedom? Was *he* at peace when his hard work and punishments were over, and this island his at last?

I've often wondered, and so I've looked for him today, hoping to find out. I've flown over the sands and peered into the cave that used to be his prison, thinking perhaps I'd see him dragging his logs as he always did. But I haven't managed to find him, and now it's time I flew off, for evening's come and there are a thousand other places I want to be.

Shall I tell you what I think, though? I don't think Caliban did change; because Caliban didn't *need* to change. I'm sure that he's somewhere on this island right now, catching fish in a stream, opening oysters with his claws, or simply sitting with his feet in a warm rock pool, gazing at the clouds' reflections and humming a melody from long ago. And if he's humming it tunelessly, you can be sure he knows how it *should* sound. He remembers how I sang it, and that's the way he's hearing it in his head.

But there's one more person who *did* change. Do you know who it is?

It's someone who saw the tempest, and heard my music, and saw all my spriting. It's someone who, from this day onwards, can see me if they simply shut their eyes. Then, they can be whisked back to this island in the twinkling of an eye, and when they're here they can swim, or dive into the fire, or ride on the curled clouds with me. It's someone who's understood the story of *The Tempest*, and who knows that everything is possible if you are free to use that one magical power that you possess: your imagination.

For Ariel changes everyone he meets; and – believe me – he's changed *you*, too.

About the Author

Franzeska G. Ewart was born in Galloway. She now lives in Glasgow, but still likes to spend time by the sea, lochs and rivers of south-west Scotland, which were an inspiration to her as she prepared this retelling of *The Tempest*.

Franzeska writes for all ages. Her *The Pen-pal From Outer Space* and *Shadowflight* were both Guardian Book of the Week. She has written three books for A & C Black, all about Bryony Bell and her meteoric rise to stardom. Bryony's proving very popular with ten year olds, and Franzeska spends much of her time demonstrating the magic tricks from *Under the Spell of Bryony Bell*. These include sawing a lady in half, which is a particular favourite!

When she's not writing, Franzeska loves to play treble recorder and look after her two cats, Lily and The Woozle.

Other White Wolves Shakespeare...

Macbeth

retold by **Tony Bradman**

One dark and stormy night, three
strange old women tell Macbeth that
he will become king! Of course it's
not possible, but their words give
Macbeth a terrifying idea. If he
kills King Duncan, he could seize
the throne for himself. Murder most
foul – if only it were that simple...

Macbeth is a modern retelling of
Shakespeare's most chilling play.

ISBN: 978 0 7136 7922 9   £4.99

Other White Wolves Shakespeare...

ROMEO & JULIET

retold by **Michael Cox**

Trouble is brewing on the roughest
estate in Nottingham. Romeo
Montague has fallen for Juliet Capulet.
Big time. But their families hate each
other's guts. Worse still, Romeo has just
killed Juliet's cousin in a street fight
and must leave town quick. What's
needed now is a clever plan…

Romeo and Juliet is a modern retelling
of a tragic Shakespeare play.

ISBN: 978 0 7136 8136 9   £4.99

Year 5

The Path of Finn McCool • Sally Prue

The Barber's Clever Wife • Narinder Dhami

Taliesin • Maggie Pearson

Fool's Gold • David Calcutt

Time Switch • Steve Barlow and Steve Skidmore

Let's Go to London! • Kaye Umansky

Year 6

Shock Forest and Other Stories • Margaret Mahy

Sky Ship and Other Stories • Geraldine McCaughrean

Snow Horse and Other Stories • Joan Aiken

Macbeth • Tony Bradman

Romeo and Juliet • Michael Cox

The Tempest • Franzeska G. Ewart